Ladybird books are widely available, but in case of
difficulty may be ordered by post or telephone from:

Ladybird Books – Cash Sales Department
Littlegate Road Paignton Devon TQ3 3BE
Telephone 01803 554761

A catalogue record for this book is available
from the British Library

Published by Ladybird Books Ltd Loughborough Leicestershire UK
LADYBIRD and the device of a Ladybird are trademarks of Ladybird Books Ltd

DISNEY

Cinderella

Ladybird

Once upon a time, in a faraway land, there lived a rich, widowed gentleman and his beautiful daughter, Cinderella.

Cinderella's father was kind and loving. He married for a second time so that his daughter had a mother to care for her.

Cinderella's stepmother had two mean and ugly daughters called Anastasia and Drizella.

5

When Cinderella's father died, her stepmother stopped pretending to like her. She was jealous of Cinderella's charm and beauty so she forced the young girl to become a servant in her own home.

Cinderella was given a tiny bedroom in the attic. Her only friends were the birds and mice. They listened as she sang about her dreams of a life filled with love and happiness.

One morning, Cinderella found a
tubby little mouse caught in a trap.
"We'll call you Gus," she said. Then
she gently set him free and put him
with the other mice for safety. "Don't
forget to warn him about Lucifer!"
Cinderella reminded them. And off
she went to begin the day's chores.

Lucifer was her stepmother's cat. He was sly and lazy, and all the animals hated him, especially Bruno the dog.

After Cinderella had given Lucifer his milk, she walked out into the yard. "Breakfast time!" she called, scattering corn for the chickens.

The mice came running for some breakfast too. But Lucifer was blocking the way to the corn. One of the mice, Jaq, crept bravely up to Lucifer and kicked him. There was a loud – SPLASH! The cat had fallen into his milk bowl.

This made Lucifer *very* angry. When he saw Gus busily gathering up some of the corn, he pounced on him...

Luckily, Gus managed to escape to the kitchen. He scampered up onto a table top where he rested against a teacup. Suddenly, the cup flipped over, trapping Gus underneath.

Just then, a voice shrieked from upstairs. "Cinderella!"

"I'm coming," Cinderella sighed. She picked up the breakfast trays and made her way upstairs. Under the teacup, Gus was safe at last.

Not far away, in the royal palace, the King and the Grand Duke were talking about the Prince.

"It's time he married," grumbled the King. Suddenly, he had an idea. "We'll have a ball – tonight!" he cried. "And invite every young maiden in the kingdom. The Prince will surely fall in love with *one* of them!"

So, invitations were sent out that very day.

When the royal messenger delivered
the invitation to Cinderella's house,
Cinderella went to find her
stepmother. She was upstairs in the
music room listening to Anastasia
and Drizella singing.

"There's going to be a ball at the palace!" exclaimed the stepmother as she read the invitation. "Every young maiden is to attend!"

"Why, that means I can go too!" said Cinderella, hopefully.

Anastasia and Drizella shrieked with laughter at the idea, but Cinderella was determined. "Well, why not?" she asked.

Her stepmother thought for a moment, then a sly look crossed her face. "I see no reason why you can't go, *if* you get all your work done."

"I'm sure I can!" cried Cinderella, rushing upstairs to find something to wear.

She opened her wardrobe and took out one of her mother's old gowns. "It's a little old-fashioned, but I'll fix that," she said.

"Cinderella!" shrieked her stepmother.

"I'm coming," Cinderella sighed.

The mice knew that poor Cinderella would never have time to finish the dress. So they decided to work on it themselves.

They sang merrily as they cut and sewed the material. At last, the pretty dress was finished. It was trimmed with an old sash and beads which Anastasia and Drizella had thrown away.

21

Later that evening, Cinderella sadly
returned to her attic room. She had
been so busy that she hadn't had
time to get ready. Out of the
window, she watched a carriage
arrive to take her stepmother and
stepsisters to the ball.

As Cinderella turned away she suddenly saw the dress. "Surprise!" her friends cried.

"Oh, it's wonderful!" Cinderella exclaimed, hardly able to believe her eyes. In no time at all, she had slipped the dress on and was rushing downstairs to the carriage.

But when Anastasia and Drizella
saw their stepsister looking so
beautiful, they were filled with
jealousy.

"Why, you little thief!" Drizella
screamed, spotting her old beads
round Cinderella's neck. Then,
Anastasia looked at the sash. "That's
mine!" she cried, grabbing the sash
and ripping Cinderella's dress.

"Please stop!" cried Cinderella. But it was too late, her dress was ruined. She ran into the garden and flung herself down by a bench. She sobbed as if her heart would break.

Cinderella was so upset that at first she didn't see a magical swirl of light gather around her. When she looked up, an old lady was sitting on the bench.

"I'm your fairy godmother," the lady said, kindly. "Dry your tears. You can't go to the ball looking like that! Now, fetch me a pumpkin and hurry, even miracles take time!"

Minutes later, the fairy godmother
waved her magic wand over the
pumpkin. "Bibbidi-bobbidi-boo!"
she sang. The pumpkin changed into
a sparkling carriage!

"Now," said the fairy godmother,
"with an elegant carriage like that,
you simply have to have – mice!"

With that, she waved her wand over
Gus, Jaq and their friends and
changed them into proud, white
horses. Another wave of the wand
and Cinderella's horse was changed
into a coachman and Bruno the dog
was changed into a footman.

Then, with a final wave of the wand, Cinderella was dressed in a magnificent ballgown and delicate glass slippers.

"Oh, thank you!" cried Cinderella, stepping into the carriage. "It's like a dream come true!"

"I know, dear, but remember you only have until midnight," the fairy godmother warned. "On the last stroke of twelve the spell will be broken."

At the palace, Cinderella entered the glittering ballroom excitedly.

Glancing up, the Prince saw her and thought she was the most beautiful girl he had ever seen. He took Cinderella's hand and led her to the dance floor. The Prince knew that he had finally fallen in love.

Dancing in the Prince's arms, Cinderella felt as though she was floating on air.

Suddenly, she heard a clock chime. It was the first stroke of midnight…

"I must go!" Cinderella gasped as she fled through the ballroom and down the palace steps.

"Wait! You can't go now!" cried the Prince. But Cinderella didn't stop – even when she lost one of her glass slippers on the steps. She leapt into the carriage which raced away.

As the last stroke of midnight was heard, the carriage turned back into a pumpkin and Cinderella found herself dressed in rags once more. But she was still wearing a single, glass slipper.

Back at the palace, the Prince was heartbroken. He declared he would only marry the girl whose foot fitted the glass slipper he had found.

The next day, the Grand Duke began his search. Every maiden in the land would have to try on the glass slipper until he found the Prince's true love.

Meanwhile, Cinderella's stepmother had become suspicious when she heard her stepdaughter humming the music from the ball. She was determined that Cinderella would not try on the slipper. When Cinderella went up to her room, she followed her and locked the door!

At last, the Grand Duke arrived.
Anastasia and Drizella were *very*
excited. Taking their turn, they tried
to s-q-u-e-e-z-e their feet into the
tiny, glass slipper. But their feet were
much too big!

Jaq and Gus were desperate to help
Cinderella. They took the attic key
from the stepmother's pocket and
slowly pushed it up the stairs to
Cinderella's room.

Hot and tired, they finally managed
to open the door and free their friend.

Just as the Grand Duke was about to leave, Cinderella appeared. "Please wait," she called. "May I try on the slipper?"

The Grand Duke led Cinderella to a chair and called for the footman. As the footman stepped forward, the wicked stepmother tripped him up. The slipper flew through the air. There was a loud crash as it hit the floor and shattered into a thousand tiny pieces.

"Oh, no!" gasped the Duke.

"Perhaps this would help..." said Cinderella, reaching into her pocket and bringing out the other glass slipper. Her stepsisters shrieked as the delighted Duke fitted the slipper onto Cinderella's foot.

Soon afterwards, Cinderella and the Prince were married. Her friends, the mice, looked on and smiled. They knew Cinderella's dreams had finally come true!